SABAN'S

MIGHTY MORPHIN
POWER RANGERS™

THE BAD
DREAM MACHINE

By Cathy East Dubowski

A PARACHUTE PRESS BOOK

GROSSET & DUNLAP • NEW YORK

A PARACHUTE PRESS BOOK
Parachute Press, Inc.
156 Fifth Avenue
New York, NY 10010

Published by Grosset & Dunlap, Inc., a member of The Putnam &
Grosset Group, New York. GROSSET & DUNLAP is a trademark of
Grosset & Dunlap, Inc. Published simultaneously in Canada.

Creative Consultant: Cheryl Saban.

With special thanks to Cheryl Saban, Debi Young, Ban Pryor, and
Sherry Stack.

Printed in the U.S.A.
August 1994
Library of Congress Catalog Card Number: 94-77644
ISBN: 0-448-40929-1
A B C D E F G H I J

PROLOGUE

Evil forces beware. Five ordinary teenagers are about to morph into—the Mighty Morphin Power Rangers.

Their incredible powers come from Zordon, a good wizard trapped in another dimension. Zordon has given each teenager a

magic coin—a Power Morpher—
and super strength drawn from
the spirits of the dinosaurs.

When things get really tough,
the Power Rangers call upon their
Dinozords—giant robots they
drive into battle.

Power Rangers, dinosaur spirits, and amazing robots—together
these incredible forces protect
the Earth.

So—get ready. *It's morphin
time!*

CHAPTER 1

BRIIIIIIINGG!

At last! The ear-splitting final bell rang through the halls of Angel Grove High. School was over for the week, and the Weather Channel had forecast a beautiful weekend ahead.

But Trini and her best friend

Kimberly were *not* smiling as they met each other at their lockers.

Trini pulled her science book from her neatly organized locker and sighed quietly.

Kimberly dug through her locker's jumble of books and papers, headbands, scrunchies, and makeup kits. Finally she found her science book under some old gym clothes. Then she checked her shoulder-length brown hair in the mirror, slammed the locker door shut, and gave the combination lock a spin.

She made a face at her science book and quickly stuffed it into her pink backpack.

"Hey, girls, you look bummed

out!" It was their close friend Zack. His black hi-tops squeaked on the wood floor as he hip-hopped down the hall with his buddies Jason and Billy.

These five best friends were nice, normal-looking teenagers— but they shared an *outrageous* secret. Whenever danger threatened the Earth, they changed— into the Mighty Morphin Power Rangers! Together they used their secret powers to face the challenges of fighting Evil. But this weekend they faced a *really* tough challenge.

"In case you hadn't heard," Kimberly said with her hands on her hips, "there's a huge science test on Monday."

Zack just grinned. "Yeah, we know all about it."

Trini and Kimberly looked at each other in amazement. They were all pretty good students. Especially Billy—he was a real brain. But Ms. Appleby's science tests were awesomely tough. Even good students had to study like crazy to do well.

"And you're not worried?" Trini asked.

"Nope," said Jason, flashing his famous smile. "Billy's got a great plan to make *sure* we all pass."

Kimberly and Trini were definitely interested!

But so were Angel Grove's

6

biggest troublemakers, Bulk and Skull. Bulk was a great big guy with a greasy ponytail and a nasty personality. He liked to push around his skinny buddy Skull, who had dark slicked-back hair and always dressed in black. Today they were hiding around the corner, eavesdropping on what their five classmates were saying.

Billy's blue eyes twinkled behind his glasses as he revealed his plan. "We were thinking about all of us going up to my uncle's inn. It's up in the mountains. We can spend the whole weekend studying."

"If we work together on this,"

said Zack, "the test will be a breeze."

"Great idea!" Kimberly and Trini both said at once. Suddenly the weekend looked a whole lot brighter. Chattering with excitement, the five friends began to make plans.

Meanwhile, around the corner, Bulk felt someone tap him on the shoulder. He and Skull spun around as if they'd been caught stealing. It was Mr. Caplan, principal of Angel Grove High School. He was waving two large yellow index cards in their faces.

"Do you boys know what these are?" Mr. Caplan asked with a tight smile.

"Uh, early birthday cards?" Bulk guessed nervously.

"Oooh, Mr. Caplan," said Skull, shaking so hard it made his one dangly earring jingle, "you shouldn't have."

"I didn't!" Mr. Caplan said through clenched teeth. He held the yellow cards up by the corners, as if they were smelly fish. "These are your mid-semester grades."

"Ouch!" said Bulk.

"Yeah, ouch," Skull agreed.

"*Ouch* is right," the principal said with a frown. "If you two get D's on Monday's science test, you're going to spend every day for the rest of the year staying after school. Remember, D is for Detention!"

Bulk and Skull stared, speechless, as Mr. Caplan turned and walked quickly down the hall.

"Well," Skull mumbled finally, "at least we know where we'll be after school from now on."

"Don't be a dweeb!" Bulk growled. Then he grinned devilishly. "I've got a plan...." He peeked around the corner again at Billy, Trini, Kimberly, Zack, and Jason.

"We'll just follow those geeks this weekend," Bulk said with a snicker, "and let them do all the work for us."

Bulk and Skull weren't the only ones who were spying on the Power Rangers. High above Earth, Rita Repulsa watched them from her cold, gloomy fortress on the moon. A nasty smile twisted across her face as she listened to the new plan of her chief warrior, Goldar.

"This is perfect!" Goldar cried, his red eyes glowing with excitement. "With the Power Rangers all sleeping in the same place, I can finally call on the Crystal of Nightmares."

"I like the sound of that," Rita said gleefully. "But what is that, you twit?"

Goldar carefully explained how

the Crystal of Nightmares worked. "It will let us enter the Power Rangers' dreams and destroy their self-confidence...forever!"

Rita clapped her bony hands together, cackling with delight as she looked down on Earth with her cruel dark eyes.

Goldar's plan would take the power out of the Power Rangers— for good.

CHAPTER 2

At Billy's uncle's inn, birds
chirped in the cool, fresh moun-
tain air. Deer wandered peacefully
through the woods. The warm
sunlight sparkled like diamonds
on the trout-filled lake.

"This was a super-great idea,"
Kimberly said with a smile, "all of

us coming here for the weekend to study together."

Billy agreed totally. "And we've already made significant progress in preparing for the exam."

Being in the mountains was better than any of them could have imagined. Gone were all the noisy interruptions and distractions of home. They decided there was no better place to study science than surrounded by nature.

The five friends had been studying for hours in Zack, Billy, and Jason's room. Books and papers were scattered everywhere. But somehow, studying together didn't seem like hard work. They asked each other questions and discussed what they learned. That made the information seem real and alive, not just facts in a book.

At last, tall, willowy Trini stood up and stretched, flipping her long black braid over her shoulder. "I don't know about you guys, but all this studying is making me hungry. Let's take a break and get something to eat."

Laughing, the friends went in search of food.

Outside, not far from the teenagers' rooms, two heads popped up out of the bushes. It was Bulk and Skull! Bulk was using binoculars to get a close-up look at the inn. Skull was using binoculars to look up at the tree above them.

Bulk rolled his eyes. "What are you looking at, numbskull?"

"Don't move," said Skull, still looking through his binoculars. "There's a bird's nest up there."

Bulk looked up. "Where?"

Splat!

A falling egg struck Bulk on the forehead.

"There," said Skull.

Splat!

The yolk was on Skull, too.

About an hour later, a key rattled in the lock of Billy, Zack, and Jason's room. Slowly the door squeaked open.

But it wasn't Billy or Zack or Jason. It wasn't Kimberly or Trini, either.

It was just two maids—a great big one and a smaller skinny one—who had supposedly come to do their daily cleaning. Their uniforms were all twisted and wrinkled, as if they didn't fit quite right. And they were both definitely having a bad hair day!

"A-a-a-CHOO!" the big maid sneezed. "Get that feather duster out from under my nose! I'm allergic to dust!"

"Sorry, Bulk," said the skinny maid. He straightened Bulk's flipped wig for him and smiled apologetically.

"Come on, Skull," Bulk hissed. "We have to hurry. The dweebs will be back soon."

Bulk started shuffling through papers on the desk. These goody-goodies were smart, Bulk thought, and they knew how to study. There must be something here that would help him ace that test on Monday. Maybe something he could use as a cheat sheet!

He glanced over at Skull, who was still dusting...the table, the mirror. He was actually cleaning the room!

Bulk scowled. "Would you put that thing away—a-CHOO!—and help me here?"

Suddenly they froze. Voices!

Someone was coming their way!

"Good work today, you guys," they heard Jason say right outside the door. "We'll start again in the morning."

Quickly, Bulk and Skull ran to the window. But it was much too small for a big guy like Bulk to squeeze through.

Keys jingled in the lock.

Skull shot Bulk a frantic look.

The doorknob started to turn.

There was only one thing they could do. "Quick!" Bulk said, shoving Skull ahead of him.

Just then the door opened. Billy, Jason, and Zack burst in, laughing and joking around.

Everything in the room looked

the same. Their books and papers were just where they'd left them.

"Man," said Zack, "this fresh air is giving me energy to burn!" He turned on the radio by the bed. Lively music filled the room. Zack started moving to the beat.

"Hey, guys, check out this new step!"

Billy and Jason laughed as they watched Zack give new meaning to the word *dance*. He mixed hip-hop, karate, and some of his own athletic moves into what he called Hip-Hop-Kido.

Then he kicked off his shoes and began to dance on the bed.

Zack didn't know it, but his sneakers had landed two inches

from Bulk's nose. He and Skull were hiding under the bed! The trapped troublemakers moaned quietly in pain every time Zack bounced.

"Check *this* move out!" they heard Billy say. Billy grabbed a feather pillow from his bed. With a grin, he used Zack for feather pillow target practice.

"Pillow fight!" Jason shouted and joined in. Soon feathers were flying everywhere!

Under the bed, Bulk was half choking as dust and pillow feathers swirled up around his face. Skull stuck his finger under Bulk's nose, trying to keep him from sneezing. Bulk groaned—but very quietly. Would these guys ever go to bed?

The Power Rangers had no idea they'd been followed. And they certainly didn't know Bulk and Skull were trapped beneath Zack's bed. If they had known, they would have just laughed. Bulk and Skull's troublemaking was usually pretty harmless.

But what Rita Repulsa was planning for the Power Rangers was no laughing matter.

Rita had sent Goldar to Earth, to a secret cave hideout in the desert. The cave was called the Cavern of Destruction. Now Goldar paced the dirt floor, staring at a blue crystal ball in the center of the cold, dark hideout.

Raising his sword, Goldar cried out in his haunting, beastlike voice, "Crystal of Nightmares! I command you! I alone will use your powers to destroy my enemies."

Strange blue lightning crackled from his sword to the crystal. The mysterious crystal ball began to glow as its evil powers awakened.

"Pleasant dreams, do-gooders!" Goldar shouted with excitement. Electricity crackled around the Crystal of Nightmares as it sent its blue light streaking through the night.

Goldar laughed. "Soon your

dreams will turn into nightmares, and your powers will be lost forever!"

Trini closed her science book and placed it on the nightstand. She yawned and pulled the covers up to her chin. "Good night, Kimberly."

"Good night, Trini," Kimberly said. She turned off the light and curled up with her pillow. "Sweet dreams."

Both girls smiled as they closed their eyes and peacefully drifted off to sleep.

A little while later, in their own room, Jason, Billy, and Zack turned out the lights and went to sleep, too. They slept so soundly they didn't even hear the snores beneath Zack's bed. Still dressed in their maids' uniforms and wigs, Bulk and Skull were sleeping like babies.

A blue light passed over the peaceful faces of Billy, Zack, and Jason. Frowns creased their foreheads, and they began to stir in their sleep.

The blue light passed over the faces of Bulk and Skull, too, as they snored beneath Zack's bed.

In the girls' room, Trini and Kimberly began to toss and turn as their faces were bathed in the same strange, eerie glow.

The Crystal of Nightmares had begun to work its evil magic.

CHAPTER 3

Billy broke out into a cold sweat as he tossed and turned in his sleep. He was dreaming...

Dreaming that as the Blue Ranger, he was fighting a monster. He called on his special powers. He struggled to use every ounce of his intelligence, but he was totally powerless against the evil creature.

Zack was dreaming, too...

Dreaming that as the Black Ranger, he was surrounded by enemies. He defended himself with superpowers and hip-hop karate moves, but somehow he knew that he could not win.

Beneath Zack's bed, Bulk and Skull were snoring away.

Bulk was dreaming about a huge hamburger. "Burgasaurus!" he mumbled in his sleep.

Skull was dreaming about a hot dog with all the works. "Doga-saurus!" he muttered, smacking his lips.

But as the blue light passed

over their faces, their dreams changed. Now they were dressed as superheroes—and ready to save the world!

Meanwhile in the girls' room, Kimberly was dreaming...

Dreaming that as the Pink Ranger, her enemies were chasing her through a tunnel with no end, no escape.

Trini was dreaming that as the Yellow Ranger, she had lost control of all her powers, and that she could do nothing to stop the monsters that were trying to destroy Angel Grove.

Jason's nightmare was perhaps the worst.

As the Red Ranger, he should

have been able to stop Rita's newest monster. But in his dream, no matter how hard he tried, he was losing the fight. Even worse, he knew that he was failing his friends when they needed him most. The Power Rangers were about to be defeated...forever.

Then Billy, Jason, Zack, Kimberly, and Trini began to have the *same* dream at the *same* time.

They dreamed they were in their regular school clothes, standing in a circle of flickering lights. They looked up and saw a pale face wavering in a column of eerie green light—it looked as though it were underwater. It was Zordon, Rita's enemy, the good

Billy has a great weekend plan! He and his friends will study for the big science test up in the mountains.

Goldar has a plan, too—to destroy the Power Rangers' self-confidence with the Crystal of Nightmares!

Trini dreamed that she lost all her super-powers!

Kimberly dreamed that her enemies chased her through a tunnel with no end!

In Jason's dreams, no matter how hard he tried, he couldn't defeat the forces of Evil!

Bulk and Skull both dreamed they were superheroes!

Billy, Kimberly, and Trini are worried—all the Power Rangers have lost their self-confidence!

The Power Rangers teleport to the Cavern of Destruction, where the evil crystal rests.

Putty attack! Jason fights off a Putty so he can enter the cave.

Trini is usually calm and brave in the face of Putty danger—but not today!

A Putty sends Zack flying in the air!

With the evil Crystal of Nightmares destroyed, the Power Rangers wipe out the Putties!

wizard who had given them their powers. The Power Rangers were dreaming that they had been brought to his secret Command Center.

"Power Rangers!" Zordon said in a voice full of anger and disappointment. "It has become obvious that you are no longer capable of performing your duties. I have no choice but to strip you of your powers...forever!"

Suddenly, one by one, Zack, Billy, and Jason sat bolt upright in their beds, jerked from their nightmares. They were out of breath and covered in sweat.

Trini and Kimberly also awoke with a start. They sat up in their beds, unsure of what was real and what was a dream.

Knock! Knock!

Kimberly jumped at the sound, then pulled on her robe and tiptoed over to the door. It was Jason, Zack, and Billy. Quickly, she let them in.

For a moment the five friends looked at one another in silence. Each one was thinking, *What's going on?*

At last Jason spoke, his voice barely a whisper. "Did you guys have the nightmare, too?"

"Oh, no," said Kimberly as they all nodded their heads. "It was horrible!"

"Truly disturbing," said Billy.

Then they sat down and talked about what they had dreamed.

Meanwhile, Zordon watched from his Command Center.

"I have been fearing this for a long time," Zordon said to the little robot Alpha 5, who ran the Command Center. "Goldar has called upon the evil Crystal of Nightmares to destroy the Power Rangers' self-confidence."

"Aye-yi-yi-yi-yi!" squeaked Alpha 5. "What are we going to do?"

"We must summon them immediately," Zordon replied.

Back in the girls' room, the five teenagers—still upset by their nightmares—jumped as their communicators all went off at the same time.

"Oh, no," said Kimberly, nervously twisting a corner of her pink robe. "It's Zordon!"

Zack shook his head. "Man, I'm really not ready for one of Rita's monsters right now."

"Me neither," said Trini, hugging a pillow.

Billy pushed his glasses up on his nose. "I don't know if I'll *ever* be ready again."

No one wanted to be the first to answer Zordon's call.

Jason sighed. "All right, we're all scared. But we have to answer." At last he spoke into the communicator on his wrist.

"Zordon, this is Jason."

Zordon's voice echoed as if it were underwater. "I am aware of the terrible nightmares you had."

The Power Rangers looked at one another, embarrassed that Zordon knew their secret fears.

Billy finally admitted out loud what they had all been thinking. "Zordon...I'm afraid we've completely lost confidence in our abilities."

"This is exactly Goldar and Rita's plan," Zordon said. "Goldar has called upon the Crystal of Nightmares to destroy your self-confidence. And without self-confidence, your special powers are completely useless."

"So that's what's going on," said Zack, shaking his head in disgust. "We're through."

"Fortunately," Zordon continued, "Alpha 5 has located the Crystal of Nightmares that Goldar used to control your minds. You must destroy it. That will release you from your fears."

"No way," said Kimberly. "I'm hanging up my communicator."

"I don't know if we can do it," Jason admitted.

"You can and you will," Zordon said firmly. "Believe only *that* and you will succeed."

Suddenly the Power Rangers could feel something happening to them. They recognized the tingling feeling. Zordon was using his powers to transport them.

What they didn't know was— where was Zordon sending them?

Five balls of colored light—
one red, one yellow, one pink, one
blue, and one black—streaked
across the sky.

Moments later the lights shimmered, then turned into Jason,
Trini, Kimberly, Billy, and Zack.
They were dressed in their regu-

lar clothes—jeans and T-shirts and sneakers. They shook their heads to clear their thoughts, then looked around.

They were somewhere that was rocky and deserted. Zack peered over a huge rock. Several feet away was the entrance to a cave. And the cave was heavily guarded.

"Oh, great!" said Zack. "Putties!"

The place was swarming with Rita's Putty Patrol, mindless clay creatures Rita often sent to fight and try to weaken the Power Rangers.

"The Crystal of Nightmares must be inside the cave," Billy said.

"We don't stand a chance!" Trini said with a worried frown.

Kimberly was already walking away. "I'm getting out of here, you guys. Let me know how it turns out."

Suddenly another group of Putties appeared right in front of her, blocking her escape. There was no other choice. The Power Rangers would have to stand and fight.

The Power Rangers had been forced into combat with the Putties many times before. Usually they beat the dull-witted Putties because the Power Rangers were a whole lot smarter.

But today was different—

because today the Power Rangers were different. The Crystal of Nightmares had robbed them of their greatest weapon: their self-confidence.

Kimberly and Zack did their best to block the Putties' kicks and punches. But in their hearts they no longer believed they could defeat the Putties, and so they didn't even try some of their special attack moves.

"They've never been this strong before," cried Zack.

"Or this ugly!" added Kimberly.

A handful of Putties pinned Trini and Billy to a tree.

Trini was usually calm and brave in the face of danger. Not

today. "Help!" she cried out with a frightened voice.

"This is most unfortunate," Billy said, ducking his head.

Jason was trying to fight off several Putties at once. Suddenly he realized he was near the entrance to the cave.

His mind told him it was hopeless. The Power Rangers could never win. They were totally washed up.

But then something deep inside him fought that feeling of defeat. He had to keep trying. He just had to!

"Hang on, Rangers!" Jason shouted to his struggling friends. "I'm going for it!"

Jason managed to slip free and duck inside the cave. Then he stopped, staring in wonder. The glowing Crystal of Nightmares was as beautiful as it was evil. Jason could not take his eyes off it. Slowly he reached his hand out to touch it.

Suddenly Goldar stepped from the shadows. His red eyes glowed like burning coals as he moved toward Jason. He looked stronger and more evil than ever.

Was Jason's terrible nightmare about to come true? Was this really going to be the end of the Power Rangers?

CHAPTER 5

Jason was trapped. He was unarmed and all alone. How could he hope to fight Rita Repulsa's greatest warrior?

Goldar was coming toward him now. *Quick! Do something!* an inner voice told him.

Then his eyes sparkled as he

got an idea. Slowly Jason backed up toward the wall. "All right, you goon!" he shouted at Goldar. "Come and get me!"

"My pleasure!" Goldar cried. He lunged for Jason with all his strength.

Jason lurched to the side, rolling across the ground.

Instead of hitting Jason, Goldar smacked headfirst into the hard wall of the cave. For a moment he saw stars and then stumbled to his knees.

Jason knew he had only seconds. He ran toward the Crystal of Nightmares and struck it with a powerful side kick. The crystal smashed against the wall and exploded in a shower of sparks.

Far off in the Command Center, Alpha 5 and Zordon watched.

"They did it!" Alpha 5 cried, spinning in circles, with lights blinking on and off. "The Power Rangers destroyed the Crystal of Nightmares!"

Zordon smiled proudly, as if there had never been any doubt.

Back in the cave, Jason pulled himself to his feet.

Then something strange happened. A picture filled his mind—almost like a dream, even though he wasn't asleep.

In the vision Jason saw himself as the Red Ranger, defeating a monster. He raised his hand in a sign of victory.

Outside the cave, the other Power Rangers were still surrounded by Putties. But something strange was happening to them, too.

Kimberly and Zack stared for a moment as a dream image filled their minds. Kimberly saw herself as the Pink Ranger, flipping a Putty over her shoulder. Zack saw himself as the Black Ranger, fighting off a monster twice his size.

Billy and Trini were still pinned against a tree. But both stared into space as dreams filled their minds—Billy as the Blue Ranger, Trini as the Yellow Ranger, saving the Earth from Evil.

The power of the Crystal of Nightmares had been destroyed. Now the Power Rangers' minds were filled with visions of success. What a difference it made. They faced the Putties with new self-confidence.

Kimberly and Zack advanced on the Putties that had cornered them—and sent them flying.

"Catch you later, Putties!" Kimberly shouted with a smile.

"Yeah, *pasta la pizza!*" Zack cracked.

Then they hurried to help Billy and Trini. Jason ran from the cave and joined in the battle. Together they fought off the Putties with karate, gymnastics...and the strength and confidence that they'd always shared.

Within minutes the Putties had vanished.

"Good work, Rangers!" Jason said.

"I believe we've regained our self-confidence," Billy said.

"All right!" Trini cried.

The Power Rangers were their old selves again.

Up on the moon, Rita Repulsa was her old self again, too—evil, cranky, and screaming at everyone in sight!

"Why do I even bother with you?" she shrieked at Goldar.

"Those twerps smashed the Crystal of Nightmares," Goldar

whined. "What was I supposed to do?"

Then Rita's evil eyes fell on Scorpina, another of her warriors. "I know—I'll send Scorpina! By the time she's finished with them, their old nightmares will seem like sweet dreams!"

CHAPTER

6

"Well, guys," Jason said as he brushed the dust from his red jeans, "we've sent those Putties packing. Maybe we should go back to the inn and pack, too."

"Great idea," said Trini. "We might even have time left to study some more."

But suddenly Goldar and Scorpina appeared, their golden armor glinting in the bright sun. Goldar held back—Rita wanted this to be Scorpina's fight. But still he held his sword ready as he watched Scorpina instantly change—into a giant scorpion. Her two huge pincers opened and closed, and her poisonous tail lashed wildly.

Jason stepped forward. "No more fooling around, Rangers. It's morphin time!" he cried.

The air crackled with electricity as the Power Rangers raised their Power Morphers to the sky. Just as Zordon had taught them, they called upon the spirits of the ancient dinosaurs.

"Mastodon!" cried Zack.

"Pterodactyl!" cried Kimberly.

"Triceratops!" cried Billy.

"Saber-toothed Tiger!" cried Trini.

"Tyrannosaurus!" cried Jason.

In a flash, the five teenagers from Angel Grove morphed into Power Rangers!

Now they stood dressed in shining helmets and sleek jumpsuits—five powerful protectors. Jason, the Red Ranger. Kimberly, the Pink Ranger. Zack, the Black Ranger. Trini, the Yellow Ranger. And Billy, the Blue Ranger.

The Power Rangers locked hands, uniting their strength.

Then together they faced Scorpina. "Let's send her back with her tail between her legs!" Jason shouted.

Scorpina lashed out with her powerful claws. She struck with her deadly tail. But she couldn't compete with the Power Rangers, and soon she went down in a heap.

Goldar looked at Scorpina lying in the dirt. He shifted his gaze to the strong and confident Power Rangers.

With a whimper, Goldar disappeared in a flash of light.

"Sweet dreams!" the Power Rangers called after him. Then they laughed and gave each other high fives.

There was no doubt about it. The Power Rangers were back!

Back at the inn, a real maid went into one of the guest rooms to clean. She hummed to herself as she vacuumed the room. But when she tried to clean under one of the beds, her vacuum cleaner hit something big and lumpy.

She pulled up the bedspread and peeked.

"EEEEEEEEK!" she cried.

Bulk and Skull scrambled out. They were half-asleep, still dressed in their maid uniforms and wigs—and completely covered with dust. "A-a-a-CHOO!"

Bulk sneezed so hard he blew both their wigs off.

The maid shrieked again.

Now Bulk was completely awake. Suddenly he remembered. "The test! Come on, Skull—let's get out of here!"

On Monday, Jason, Trini, Billy, Kimberly, and Zack tackled Ms. Appleby's science test. The extra studying they had done really paid off. They finished the test in record time.

The next day in science class, they found Principal Caplan at the front of the room.

"Ms. Appleby is ill today," he said. "I thought I'd fill in for her so I could deliver these test results personally." Slowly, he walked up and down the aisles, passing out their graded science tests.

One by one, the five friends looked at their test papers.

"Congratulations," Mr. Caplan said. "You all got A's."

"All right!" Zack shouted.

"Wow," said Kimberly, smiling at her big red A—and then at her friends. "Studying together really paid off."

Mr. Caplan had handed back all but two of the papers. He walked back to Ms. Appleby's desk, then turned and glared. "You two—" he pointed to Bulk and Skull, "get up here."

Nervously, they went to the front of the room. Mr. Caplan handed them their tests. Each was marked with a big red F.

"Hey, Bulk!" Skull cried. "The plan worked! We didn't get D's—that means no detention!"

Bulk scowled at Skull and said through clenched teeth, "You—you d-dumb *skull!*"

Mr. Caplan cleared his throat. "Do you know what F stands for, gentlemen?"

"Uh…fun?" Bulk guessed hopefully.

"Far out?" Skull tried.

The principal walked to the blackboard and wrote *FOREVER*.

"Forever," Mr. Caplan read. "Which is how long you're going to be staying after school in my office."

"Uh, that was my next guess," Bulk mumbled.

Mr. Caplan erased the board with a few angry swishes. "I'm very disappointed in you, gentlemen," he said as he slammed the chalky eraser down on the desk. A big cloud of chalk dust rose into Bulk's face.

The chalk dust tickled Bulk's nose. "A-a-a—"

Mr. Caplan looked puzzled. "What's the matter with him?"

"Take cover!" Skull shouted and dived under a desk.

Bulk let out a huge sneeze. "A-a-a-CHOOOOOOO!"

Mr. Caplan's wig sailed off his bald head.

The whole class broke into laughter as the angry principal chased Bulk and Skull out the door.

Jason, Trini, Billy, Zack, and Kimberly grinned at each other. It had been a tough week, with two tough tests: one in science, the other in confidence. It felt good to know that with teamwork, they'd aced them both.